Brer Rabbit

Brer
Rabbit

Cathay Books

First published 1982 Cathay Books
59 Grosvenor Street, London W1

Copyright © 1982 Martspress Limited
this edition copyright © 1982 Cathay Books

ISBN 0 86178 165 1

Created by Martspress Limited
Nork Way, Banstead, Surrey

Printed in Czechoslovakia
50435

Contents

How all the fun at Briar Patch began.

Things were different in the good old days. For a start, most folks lived in the countryside and grew their own food in their own back gardens. And for another thing, all the animals could talk. They could talk to each other and they could talk to human folk.

Why, a rabbit would think no more of dropping in for tea with a human family than he would think it strange to walk along chatting with a fox.

Yes they certainly did things differently in the old days.

But then things started to change. Some of the animals started to eye each other and fell to wondering how some nice roast meat would taste with the carrots they were growing in their back

to having a craze for cooking. Morning, noon and night they were trying out new cakes, new pies and new stews. And you can guess who was always round at Miss Meadows' house sampling the cooking. Why, Brer Rabbit of course!

With all this good food and fine eating, Brer Rabbit's tummy grew rounder and rounder and his fur grew sleeker and

gardens or they bought at market.

It was *then* that creatures like Brer Rabbit had to start being a mite more careful. In fact, *very* careful indeed. Brer Rabbit first noticed the change one lovely, golden summer.

That summer Miss Meadows and the girls, Brer Rabbit's special friends, fell

sleeker and he began to look pretty tasty himself.

At least that is what Brer Fox thought, who had heard of the new ideas about eating meat.

So Brer Fox set out to catch Brer Rabbit and eat him for his dinner.

Whenever Brer Rabbit went out for a

walk, there was Brer Fox hiding and watching him with greedy eyes.

Well, one afternoon, just after tea at Miss Meadows' house, where Brer Rabbit had been eating huge helpings of chocolate cake, Brer Fox dropped by and sat in the big rocking chair on the front verandah.

'Oh my, what a shame,' cried Miss Meadows. 'I declare, Brer Fox, you have just missed tea and now there is no more chocolate cake left for you.'

'Never mind, Miss Meadows,' smiled Brer Fox, looking at Brer Rabbit and licking his lips. 'I may have missed tea, but I reckon to find a mighty good supper around these parts.'

Poor Brer Rabbit shook so hard he almost fell out of his chair. But he didn't want to seem a coward in front of Miss Meadows and the girls. 'Perhaps I can sneak off while Brer Fox is chatting with Miss Meadows,' thought Brer Rabbit, so he said:

'What time are you thinking of going home, Brer Fox?'

'Just any time you are,' smiled Brer Fox, showing his sharp white teeth. 'I'll stroll along with you, Brer Rabbit, and who knows, maybe as we go along I'll find myself a tasty something for my stewpot.'

Brer Rabbit knew what that meant. That tasty something was himself. He gave up the idea of sneaking off alone.

So then Brer Rabbit said: 'You have to have good eyesight to find a good supper these days, Brer Fox. Have you got good eyesight?'

'Indeed I have,' said Brer Fox.

'Well now,' said Brer Rabbit, 'maybe you can see that smoke rising up across the fields there.' And he pointed in the direction of Brer Fox's house.

Well, there was no smoke really, but Brer Fox, who was very proud of his sharp eyesight, was certainly not going to let it seem that he couldn't see just as well as Brer Rabbit.

So Brer Fox said: 'Sure I can see smoke, Brer Rabbit.'

'It looks to me as if it were coming from your house,' said Brer Rabbit, 'and now it's getting thicker.'

Meanwhile Miss Meadows had been rubbing her eyes and looking and looking. She was rather short-sighted, but if Brer Rabbit and Brer Fox both said they could see smoke, then she believed smoke there must be.

'Why, Brer Fox, how can you sit there so calm and quiet while your house is on fire?' she gasped. 'You must run home at once to help your wife.'

Brer Fox shifted around uncomfortably. He could not quite think how, but he felt he was being tricked. Miss Meadows dragged him off the verandah by the scruff of his neck.

'For shame!' she cried. 'You can see smoke coming from the direction of your home and yet you stay dallying here. Come with me and we will both go to help your wife.'

Down the road they raced, and by the time they found out there really was no fire, Brer Rabbit was safely in his house, with the door locked.

And after that he was mighty careful with Brer Fox.

How Brer Rabbit tricked Brer Wolf.

Now, as wise folks know, you can never depend on the weather. Sometimes it is good and sometimes it is bad.

Sometimes it is awful good and sometimes it is awful bad.

And sometimes it is worse.

Well, one year, in the part of the country where Brer Rabbit lived, the weather was terrible hard and food was very difficult to come by.

Poor old Brer Rabbit's tummy was so empty it seemed as if someone was pinching it. It was the same with Brer Fox and Brer Wolf and Brer Bear and all the other animals thereabouts.

Things went on this way until one day Brer Rabbit and Brer Wolf met along the road. They had both been out looking for food for their families and they had not found one single carrot.

'Howdy!' said Brer Rabbit gloomily. 'Howdy!' growled Brer Wolf.

'Did you find anything to eat?' asked Brer Rabbit.

'Nothing,' said Brer Wolf. 'There's nothing left!'

'Oh yes, there is,' said Brer Rabbit. 'But you have to buy it, not find it like we always do.'

'Well, you may be right,' said Brer Wolf. 'But I haven't any money, have you?'

'No,' said Brer Rabbit.

And they both walked along sadly for a while.

Then Brer Rabbit had an idea.

'We'll sell something,' he said. 'Some furniture. We can take it to market tomorrow.'

'That's a good idea,' said Brer Wolf, brightening a little.

So next day, Brer Wolf loaded up some pieces of his furniture and Brer Rabbit loaded up some of his. And off they went to market.

They sold their furniture and they bought a cartload of good food. Then they set off home.

On the way, Brer Wolf began to think to himself: 'I am bigger than Brer Rabbit and I am stronger than Brer Rabbit. What am I doing, sharing this food with him? I'll take *all* the food and what's more I'll have Brer Rabbit for my stew-pot as well.'

Well now, Brer Rabbit was no fool. It didn't take him long to guess what Brer Wolf was thinking, so he began to make his own plans.

They were driving through the woods and the road was wet and muddy because it had been raining for days.

Brer Rabbit said, 'There is a patch of wild onions growing in that wood. I'll go and see if there are any ready for eating.'

'Don't worry,' said Brer Wolf, greedy as ever. 'I'll go and see.'

As soon as he had disappeared from sight, Brer Rabbit drove the cart off the road and hid it among the trees.

Then he cut off a bit of hair from each of the horses' tails and stuck the hair in some mud holes in the road.

Brer Wolf came galloping back. 'I can't find any onions, Brer Rabbit.' he said.

'I guess they haven't grown yet,' said Brer Rabbit. 'And look what happened to the cart, Brer Wolf. You can't see it at all now, except for the horses' tails sticking up.'

Brer Wolf was mighty surprised. 'Oh my,' he said. 'But if we pull together, we should be able to pull up the horses, the cart and the food.'

For a moment Brer Rabbit's heart sank. He hadn't bargained on Brer Wolf saying that. He had thought Brer Wolf was too stupid.

Brer Rabbit did some mighty quick thinking and then he smiled and said, 'Yes indeed, we should be able to manage that.'

And he took hold of one horse's tail and Brer Wolf took hold of the other horse's tail – or so he thought. Really he was just taking hold of a piece of tail stuck in the mud.

Then both Brer Rabbit and Brer Wolf heaved mightily, and of course the pieces of tail came up out of the mud lickety-split.

'Why!' gasped Brer Rabbit, pretending to be astonished. 'We've pulled the horses' tails right off.'

'Landsakes!' gasped Brer Wolf. 'Now we shall never get the cart out of the mud. Without the tails to guide us, we just shan't know where it is.'

And that was exactly what Brer Rabbit wanted Brer Wolf to think.

Well, Brer Wolf stood around for a while, but he didn't know what to do, so in the end he just slouched off home.

Crafty Brer Rabbit waited until Brer Wolf was well out of sight, and then he went into the bushes where he had hidden the horses and the cart loaded with all the lovely food.

Then he drove the cart home to his own family – and how well they ate.

Beads for Miss Meadows.

When Brer Rabbit went to visit Miss Meadows and the girls one afternoon, he found them all parading around and showing off their new beads.

'Those are mighty fine beads,' said Brer Rabbit. 'Where did you find them?'

'Why, we made them,' replied Miss Meadows with a big smile.

'Made them?' asked Brer Rabbit.

'Yes, we did indeed,' said Miss Meadows and the girls proudly. 'Out of water melon seeds.'

'We don't like to eat water melon much, but we sure would like some more seeds to make bracelets to match our necklaces,' one of the girls giggled.

Well, Brer Rabbit just happened to know that Brer Fox was growing a fine water melon in his garden. So he told Miss Meadows about it.

Miss Meadows said, 'Brer Rabbit, do you think Brer Fox will let us have the seeds when he eats his water melon.'

Brer Rabbit thought Brer Fox might just do that. He also thought it would be mighty nice to eat that melon himself, and not wait till Brer Fox ate it.

So he bowed politely to Miss Meadows and the girls and then kicked up his heels and was away over the hill to Brer Fox's house.

Brer Fox was in his garden, looking at his water melon. He sure felt proud of that water melon. It was the biggest and greenest water melon he had ever grown. Brer Fox was very, very fond of water melon.

So when Brer Rabbit came lolloping along, Brer Fox naturally made sure to guard his water melon. He knew Brer Rabbit was fond of melon too.

'Howdy, Brer Fox,' said Brer Rabbit.

'Howdy, Brer Rabbit,' said Brer Fox. 'Kindly don't come any nearer my water melon if you don't mind.'

'I don't want your old water melon,' said Brer Rabbit. 'But I know that Miss Meadows and the girls would like it. They have a real fancy for water melon right now and they can't seem to lay their hands on a water melon at all, no indeed they can't.'

Already Brer Rabbit wasn't telling the absolute, straight through truth.

Well, Brer Fox couldn't make up his mind. On one hand he just loved water melon and on the other hand he liked to keep in with Miss Meadows and the girls, on account of them being such mighty fine cooks. He thought mighty hard.

'I don't know,' Brer Fox said doubtfully. 'I like Miss Meadows well enough, but I sure was looking forward to eating this water melon myself.'

And Brer Rabbit said, 'Well, Miss Meadows might ask you round to dinner if you gave her a present like that water melon.'

Brer Fox muttered a bit and grumbled a bit more and then he made up his mind. He put his water melon in his wheelbarrow and off he went to Miss Meadows' house.

'Miss Meadows, I would like you to accept this water melon as a present,' said Brer Fox politely.

Well, you can imagine that Miss Meadows was puzzled and surprised. She started to say, 'But I only want the seeds,' when Brer Rabbit came bustling along.

'That sure is nice of you, Brer Fox,' said Brer Rabbit. 'I guess Miss Meadows is very happy to have your water melon.' And he gave everyone a big, big smile.

Then Brer Fox went home and Brer Rabbit went most of the way with him, just so Brer Fox didn't get any fancy ideas about Brer Rabbit eating the water melon.

But the very next day, Brer Rabbit was round at Miss Meadows' house again.

Naturally, Miss Meadows and the girls were surprised to see Brer Rabbit again so soon, but they acted hospitable-like and invited him in.

Well, after saying, 'Howdy?' and enquiring real polite about the health of all Miss Meadows' folks, Brer Rabbit said: 'I thought maybe I would come a-visiting to help you out with that water melon problem you have.' Brer Rabbit paused expectantly, hoping that Miss Meadows would offer him some water melon straight away, but she didn't. She just looked at Brer Rabbit as if she were thinking mighty deep thoughts – *mighty* deep.

So Brer Rabbit smiled a real bright smile and went on, 'I know you and the girls don't much like to eat water melon, but *I* sure like water melon – and if you can't manage to eat all that great big melon that Brer Fox brought round the other day, then I don't mind helping you out by eating some. I don't mind at all. Always try to help your neighbour, that's what I say.'

After a long, long pause, Miss Meadows said, 'Why, thank you kindly, Brer Rabbit, that's right friendly of you.' And she took the seeds out and gave the water melon to Brer Rabbit to eat.

But Miss Meadows was no fool, and she guessed that Brer Rabbit had been up to his trickery again.

So the very next Sunday, when she and the girls were wearing their melon-seed necklaces and bracelets, they invited Brer Fox to dinner and gave him the best meal they had ever cooked.

Brer Fox enjoyed the meal even more than he would have enjoyed his water melon, so he was happy.

But it was lucky he never found out who really had eaten the water melon – yes indeed it was.

Brer Rabbit flies a kite.

Every few months, in the land where the animals lived, there was a big market down in the meadow.

There were stalls for clothes, for food, for pots and pans and even stalls for toffee apples.

Well, one day during the week before the big market was to be held, Mrs Rabbit said to Brer Rabbit, 'I must take the little rabbits to the market next week and buy them their new winter jackets. And I thought maybe we could all have a lovely, sticky toffee apple each while we're there.'

As soon as the little rabbits heard the words 'toffee apple' they jumped around with excitement.

And every morning for the next week, they sang out, 'We want toffee apples.'

'Daddy Rabbit will buy us toffee apples,' said one little rabbit.

'We can't wait for market day!' cried another.

Now it happened that Brer Fox had been finding it pretty hard to get food lately. He had taken to hanging around near Brer Rabbit's house, watching the little rabbits with a hungry gleam in his eye.

So, when the day of the market drew near, Brer Rabbit tried to think of a way of getting himself and Mrs Rabbit and all the little rabbits safely out of the house and to market, without being caught by hungry Brer Fox.

When he could see Brer Fox hiding outside behind a tree, Brer Rabbit went out and walked up and down.

Then he said, as if he were talking to himself, but making quite sure that Brer Fox could hear. 'I know what to do. I'll make a big kite and put each of my little rabbits in a sack and tie the sacks to the kite string. Then I'll fly the kite high above the trees, and hold the string tightly and run to the market.

'That crazy old Brer Fox will never guess that my little rabbits are hidden in the sacks,' finished Brer Rabbit in a good loud voice.

Brer Fox, who had heard every word, chuckled to himself. 'Brer Rabbit is a fool if he thinks he can trick me with a silly idea like that,' he said.

So on the day of the big market, Brer Rabbit ran out of his house, holding the string of a big kite. And hanging from the kite string were lots of bulging sacks, bulging just the way they would if little rabbits were inside.

Along the road ran Brer Rabbit, holding the kite string and the kite flew high above the trees. Then who should step out from the bushes, but Brer Fox.

'Howdy!' said Brer Fox.

'Howdy!' said Brer Rabbit, still running, but running much faster now.

'What have you got in those sacks, Brer Rabbit?' asked Brer Fox, running alongside Brer Rabbit.

'Nothing to interest you, Brer Fox, just some old rags. Nothing but old rags,' said Brer Rabbit.

'Are you sure it's old rags up there?' asked Brer Fox.

'Absolutely certain,' said Brer Rabbit.

'I don't believe you,' said Brer Fox. 'I think your little rabbits are in those sacks.'

'You are wrong,' said Brer Rabbit. 'What would my little rabbits be in those sacks for?'

Brer Fox wasted no more time. He knew how tricky Brer Rabbit was, and he didn't intend to be outwitted this time. He grabbed at the kite string and tried to pull it out of Brer Rabbit's hands.

Of course, Brer Rabbit acted like he didn't want to let go. There was a mighty scuffling and struggling. And between all the pushing and pulling, the kite string slipped through both their hands and in a moment the kite was drifting off.

Away sailed the kite across the fields, with the sacks still hanging from its string trailing underneath.

Brer Rabbit pretended to be mighty upset.

'Oh my poor little rabbits! What will become of them!' he wailed.

He sobbed and shrieked and declared that he would never see his little rabbits again, and that they would be blown fair over to China, they would – and how would they manage, not speaking a word of the language? A fine fuss Brer Rabbit surely did make.

But Brer Fox wasted no time in saying how upset he was. With a mighty growl, he ran after the kite and grabbed at the string as it danced along just a few feet from the ground.

He chased it for miles and miles, over fields and through streams, till he was quite worn out.

Then, at last, the wind dropped and Brer Fox caught the kite string.

When he hauled down the kite and opened the sacks, just guess what he found – *old rags!*

Brer Rabbit had fooled him again.

But, of course, by this time Mrs Rabbit had sneaked out with the baby rabbits and met Brer Rabbit at the fair and bought the jackets and toffee apples, and they were safely home again.

Brer
Rabbit
talks
about
giant
carrots

Brer Rabbit, as we all know, was a mighty clever little rabbit.

But one summer it seemed that he had forgotten how to be smart and started to be silly.

It began one day when he was walking past Brer Bear's carrot patch.

Brer Bear's carrots were growing fine and fat, but Brer Rabbit didn't give them a second glance.

He walked right on by and called out to Brer Bear!

'Howdy!'

'Howdy!' answered Brer Bear.

'That's mighty hard work,' smiled Brer Rabbit. 'Why do you go to so much bother for a few little carrots?'

Brer Bear stood up from his weeding and growled:

'They're bigger than *your* carrots.'

'That's what *you* think, my friend, that's what *you* think,' laughed Brer Rabbit.

And he went right on walking.

Then he went to Brer Fox's house and said the same mighty silly things about Brer Fox's carrots.

And then he went to Brer Wolf's house and said the same about Brer Wolf's carrots.

Brer Bear and Brer Fox and Brer Wolf were all mighty offended, I can tell you.

And when they heard Brer Rabbit had said just the same thing to each of them, they were mighty curious, too.

So they crept around to Brer Rabbit's house to see if his carrots really were bigger than theirs.

But they couldn't see any carrots at all.

There was Brer Rabbit's carrot patch, just where it had always been, but no sign of a carrot.

Stranger than this though, there was Brer Rabbit stirring some seeds in a wooden bowl and saying mysterious words over them.

Words that Brer Bear and Brer Fox and Brer Wolf had never heard before.

Then, almost as if he had been told to, one of the baby rabbits came running out and asked:

'Daddy Rabbit, what are you doing?'

And Brer Rabbit said, loud enough for Brer Fox and Brer Bear and Brer Wolf to hear:'These are magic carrot seeds and the magic spell I am saying will make the carrots grow so big and so fast that by midnight tonight we will have enough carrots to last us through the winter.'

'That surely is wonderful,' squealed the baby rabbit.

'Yes, that surely is wonderful,' muttered Brer Bear.

And Brer Fox and Brer Wolf agreed with him.

Then the three of them pricked up their ears again, as Brer Rabbit went on talking.

'All I have to do now is plant the seeds,' said Brer Rabbit, in that same loud voice, just as if he knew someone was listening from a little way off.

'But for that,' he went on, 'I need my magic coat. Just slip inside and fetch it for me, will you, baby rabbit. It is the black coat with the silver stars on it.'

'A magic black coat with silver stars on it – oh MY!' gasped Brer Bear, very impressed.

'Brer Rabbit must make very strong magic in a coat like that,' sighed Brer Fox.

'Yessir,' agreed Brer Wolf.

So the little rabbit ran into the house and by and by he came out again carrying the magic black coat with the silver stars.

And Brer Rabbit put on the coat and walked up and down, sowing the carrot seed and chanting magic words.

Brer Fox and Brer Bear and Brer Wolf were very impressed and made up their minds to come back at midnight, which was when Brer Rabbit had said the giant carrots would be ready.

At midnight everything round Brer Rabbit's house was very quiet.

No one came to bother Brer Fox and Brer Bear and Brer Wolf, as they dug up the carrot patch just where they had seen Brer Rabbit planting the seeds.

They dug and they dug, but they didn't find any giant carrots. They didn't even find any little carrots.

'Brer Rabbit has tricked us again,' they grumbled and wearily trudged off home.

But they were still puzzled.

They didn't understand how it could advantage Brer Rabbit to have them dig up his empty carrot patch.

They soon found out.

As they each arrived home in the dawn light, they found that all the carrots had been dug from their own carrot patches.

No wonder it had been quiet at *Brer Rabbit's* house.

Brer Rabbit had been away at *their*

houses stealing *their* carrots.

Of course they chased after Brer Rabbit, but they didn't catch him. They just saw him running indoors with the last carrot he had dug up.

Brer Rabbit had won again.

Strawberry time.

Every year, round about the time when the strawberries were ripening in the fields, each of the animals tried to be the first one to find ripe strawberries.

And every year, no matter how hard Brer Fox, Brer Bear and Brer Wolf tried, Brer Rabbit was always the first one to find the strawberries. Well, you can imagine how mad this made Brer Fox and Brer Bear and Brer Wolf.

So they decided on a plan to make Brer Rabbit give away his secret places for finding ripe strawberries.

'We will take turns to watch Brer Rabbit everywhere he goes,' said Brer Fox. 'And we'll find ripe strawberries at the same time Brer Rabbit does.'

So every time Brer Rabbit went walking, either Brer Fox, Brer Bear or Brer Wolf could be seen sneaking along behind him, but always keeping out of sight.

That made Brer Rabbit feel mighty uncomfortable. He knew that he was being followed. And, since he was the smartest animal of them all, he guessed right away *why* he was being followed.

Pretty soon, Brer Rabbit's cunning rabbity mind had worked out a way to

spot where he guessed strawberries could be found, juicy and ripe.

But he didn't eat any strawberries. Oh no, that wasn't part of his plan. He just picked two big juicy ones and put them in his pocket. Then he raced back to the road again.

By the time Brer Fox came around the corner, Brer Rabbit was strolling along the road as if he had never left it.

Brer Rabbit walked down to the river. Then he took the ladder from its hiding place and stretched it across to a little island in the middle of the river.

Brer Fox watched greedily from behind a tree as Brer Rabbit, smiling to himself, walked across the ladder on to the island.

Brer Fox didn't follow, but he sure listened hard.

He heard 'Chomp! Chomp! Chomp!'

Then he saw Brer Rabbit coming back across the ladder. And all over Brer Rabbit's whiskers were the stains of fresh strawberry juice.

At once Brer Fox went scampering off to tell Brer Wolf and Brer Bear that he had found out where Brer Rabbit picked his strawberries and they all came running to the island.

As soon as they were on the island, Brer Terrapin came along – as arranged with Brer Rabbit – and asked if he could borrow the ladder.

'Borrow it for as long as you like,' laughed Brer Fox, 'we're going to be mighty busy here on this island.'

So Brer Terrapin kept the ladder all that day and all through the night, which made Brer Fox and Brer Wolf and Brer Bear mighty mad, because they soon found there were no strawberries on the island.

But Brer Rabbit and Brer Terrapin, they sure had a mighty fine laugh!

trick the other animals.

First, he went to visit his friend, Brer Terrapin.

Next, he borrowed a ladder from Mr Man's farmyard and hid it down by the river.

Then he set out for a country walk, as if he hadn't a care in the world.

Now that morning, it was Brer Fox's turn to follow Brer Rabbit. Brer Rabbit strolled along. But when he was out of sight of Brer Fox around a bend in the road, he raced as hard as he could go to a

Brer Rabbit and the stewpot.

One summer, all the animals were head-over-tails with excitement, because the fair had come to town.

My, what fun they had on the swing-boats and the roundabouts.

Especially Brer Rabbit.

He stayed all morning at the fair, until, round about dinner time, he began to feel mighty hungry.

So off he went, lickety-clipping along the road towards home.

Now Brer Fox was feeling hungry too.

And when he saw Brer Rabbit lickety-clipping up the road, Brer Fox jumped down out of the tree he was hiding in – THUMP – right on top of Brer Rabbit, yelling as he fell.

Brer Fox was planning to turn him into tasty rabbit stew.

So he thought mighty hard and mighty fast.

'Have you been to the fair, Brer Fox?' asked Brer Rabbit.

'Indeed I have.'

'Did you see the tinker selling lovely

Brer Fox grabbed Brer Rabbit tight.

'Where are you off to, Brer Rabbit?' asked Brer Fox, thinking of the rabbit stew he could now have.

'Why, just on my way home to dinner, Brer Fox, just on my way home to dinner,' gasped Brer Rabbit.

'Come to my house, it's much nearer,' said Brer Fox, with a foxy grin.

Well now, Brer Rabbit guessed that

big pots?'

'Indeed I did.'

'I guess I should tell you that your stewpot is much too old to make tasty rabbit stew in,' said Brer Rabbit. 'So, just to prove what a good friend I am, I sure would like to buy you a new stewpot for tasty stews, Brer Fox.'

'Well now, Brer Rabbit, that is mighty nice of you,' said Brer Fox.

So back to the fair they went.

But all the time, Brer Fox kept a tight hold on Brer Rabbit. He didn't want to lose his dinner.

Brer Rabbit told the tinker that he wanted the biggest and shiniest stewpot and the tinker fetched one out.

In those days stewpots were sold by wandering tinkers, you know. Folk didn't buy their pans in shops as they do nowadays.

Anyway, Brer Rabbit said: 'I'll just make sure that the stewpot is a good fit for me, since I shall be the first bit of cooking you do in your new stewpot.'

And he smiled at Brer Fox and he jumped into the stewpot.

He scrambled around inside and then Brer Rabbit called out:

'Wonderful! Marvellous! Who would believe it?'

And that made Brer Fox feel kind of curious.

'What's so wonderful?' he asked.

Brer Rabbit popped his head over the top of the stewpot and he said:

'Why, this must be a magic pot. It shines like silver on the inside and I can see magic pictures.'

'Magic pictures?' asked Brer Fox.

'Yes, indeed,' said Brer Rabbit.

'I'd sure like to look, Brer Rabbit,' said Brer Fox.

'No, no, Brer Fox, I want to stay here and go on looking at the pictures,' replied Brer Rabbit, making out as if he wanted to stay in the stewpot for ever.

'GET OUT!' shouted Brer Fox in his fiercest, growliest voice. He didn't want to miss anything good.

So Brer Rabbit jumped out of the stew-pot as fast as he possibly could.

And Brer Fox jumped in.

Now Brer Fox was much bigger than Brer Rabbit, and the stewpot was a tight fit.

He twisted this way and he twisted that way.

It took Brer Fox quite a time to find out that the inside of the stewpot was not, after all, covered with magic pictures.

At last Brer Fox called out:

'Brer Rabbit, why can't I see the pictures?'

Naturally, there was no reply.

Because, of course, there never had been any pictures on the inside of the stewpot.

It had all been another of Brer Rabbit's clever tricks to get himself out of a jam.

As soon as Brer Fox was well crouched down in the stewpot looking for pictures that weren't there, Brer Rabbit had been lickety-clipping along the road towards his home.

And that wily little rabbit was back inside his own front door and eating his dinner before Brer Fox had even climbed back out of the stewpot.

Brer Fox felt mighty foolish at the way he had been tricked, and he asked the tinker fellow not to put the story about amongst folk.

But somehow all the other creatures got to know and a lot of giggling and smiling behind hands there was every time Brer Fox passed by.

But whether it was the tinker who told the story around, or whether it was Brer Rabbit, Brer Fox will never know.

Brer Rabbit saves the cherries.

One day when Brer Rabbit was lolloping along the road, he heard some mighty strange noises coming from Mr. Man's house.

BANG! BANG!

Then: SQUAWK! SQUAWK! SQUAWK!

So being a very inquisitive rabbit, he went to see what was happening.

He poked his nose through the fence and there was Mr. Man with his gun.

BANG! BANG!

Mr. Man fired his gun into the air.

Squawk! Squawk! A flock of birds flew up from the cherry tree.

For a while all was quiet.

Then gradually all the birds came back into the tree and started eating the cherries again.

And, of course, Mr. Man had to come out and fire his gun again.

Brer Rabbit called out to Mr. Man: 'Howdy, Mr. Man, sir.'

And Mr. Man replied: 'Howdy!'

'I see the birds are eating all your cherries, Mr. Man,' said Brer Rabbit.

'You see right, Brer Rabbit.'

'And you have many important things to do besides scaring off birds, Mr. Man,' went on Brer Rabbit.

'Right again, Brer Rabbit,' agreed Mr. Man.

'I'll scare off the birds for you,' offered Brer Rabbit. 'There's nothing in the whole world I'd rather do.'

Mr. Man roared with laughter. 'I'll bet you'd like to do just that,' he said, 'and eat all the cherries yourself at the same time.'

'I promise I won't eat a single cherry,' said Brer Rabbit. 'All I want to do is race home and tell my family I shall be busy for the day, and then I'll guard your cherries as true as true.'

So Mr. Man agreed, as he did have important things to do, and Brer Rabbit raced home and had a *very* important word with his family. Then he set out to guard the cherries.

And if Mr. Man happened to notice that Brer Rabbit's family was playing near his lettuce patch, he didn't bother none about that. He was too busy hoping that Brer Rabbit wasn't eating the cherries.

But at the end of the day the cherries were quite safe on the tree, and Mr Man was so pleased he gave Brer Rabbit a golden coin.

But he wasn't so pleased when he went to look at his lettuces. They had all been eaten by the rabbits, while Mr. Man had been thinking about the cherries.

To teach
Brer Rabbit
a lesson.

One day, when Brer Fox was walking along the road, he happened
to meet his friend, Brer Bear.
'Howdy, Brer Bear,' said Brer Fox.

'Howdy, Brer Fox' said Brer Bear, 'I
hope you are well this fine morning.'

'No, I'm not,' said Brer Fox.

'Why? Are you sick?' asked Brer Bear.

'No, I'm not sick,' replied Brer Fox.
'But I *am* sick of the way Brer Rabbit is
acting these days.'

'I can tell you,' went on Brer Fox, 'I
have never met such a small, weak and
stupid animal as that rabbit, but he acts
as if he were as big and strong and clever
as you and I, Brer Wolf.'

'I noticed Brer Rabbit has been acting
mighty biggety again,' said Brer Bear.

'And talking biggety, too,' said Brer
Fox. 'He makes me really mad, does that
Brer Rabbit.'

'He makes me mad, too,' agreed Brer

Bear.

They walked on for a while in gloomy silence.

'Let's go and visit Brer Wolf. Maybe he will have an idea about how we can teach Brer Rabbit a lesson,' said Brer Bear.

'Well now,' smiled Brer Fox. 'That's a mighty fine idea of yours, Brer Bear.'

So off they went to Brer Wolf's house.

'Howdy!' said Brer Wolf, as Brer Fox and Brer Bear came along. 'What can I do for you folk?'

'We want to teach that Brer Rabbit a lesson that he won't forget for a long time,' said Brer Bear.

'Been acting biggety again, has he?' asked Brer Wolf.

'And talking biggety too,' added Brer Fox. 'He makes us really mad, does Brer Rabbit.'

'Let's go into the woods,' said Brer Wolf, 'and find a quiet spot to have a talk.'

So the three big animals walked down the road together.

By and by they found a shady spot looking over the meadows and sat down on a log.

'We've got to fix that Brer Rabbit once and for all,' said Brer Bear.

'It's not so easy to do that as it is to talk about it,' said Brer Wolf. 'I reckon the only way to fix him once and for all would be to eat him.'

'Eat him?' said Brer Fox.

'Eat him,' said Brer Wolf.

The idea had a nice sound about it.

'It sure would stop him from being biggety,' smiled Brer Bear.

'And it would give us a free dinner,' beamed Brer Fox.

'It's an idea that will do everyone some good,' said Brer Wolf.

'What are we waiting for?' they all agreed. 'Rabbit stew for supper it is then.'

'Brer Rabbit won't talk so biggety once he is simmering in your stewpot,' said Brer Wolf to Brer Fox.

'No sir!' laughed Brer Fox and he got up and did a little happy dance right there in the meadow.

Now, while Brer Fox and Brer Wolf and Brer Bear were all laughing and chatting, they didn't hear a rustling in the bushes behind them.

And they didn't see a small brown rabbit smiling to himself.

They had no idea that Brer Rabbit was watching them.

And he had heard every word they had said.

Brer Rabbit sneaked away from there without making a sound and he thought about what he had heard.

Brer Rabbit, too, made his plans.

He didn't hide and he didn't run away.

He walked right along the road, past where Brer Fox and Brer Bear and Brer Wolf were still laughing and dancing.

'Howdy,' called Brer Rabbit politely.

'Howdy!' replied Brer Bear and Brer Fox and Brer Wolf.

Brer Rabbit looked at Brer Fox and Brer Bear and Brer Wolf.

'Well,' he said, 'I sure am glad to see that you folks can take your troubles so lightly. It surely does warm my heart.'

Brer Bear and Brer Fox and Brer Wolf were surprised.

They didn't know that they had any troubles.

But they didn't want to appear stupid.

Brer Bear cleared his throat.

'We always believe in taking troubles lightly,' he smiled, 'but what particular troubles were you referring to, Brer Rabbit?'

Brer Rabbit looked straight at Brer

31

Fox and thought for a moment.

'Well,' he said, 'Mr. Fox is being so mighty brave about his cabbages. There aren't many folks who can dance and laugh, as if they haven't a care in the world, when someone is stealing their cabbages.'

Brer Fox leapt to his feet. '*Who* is stealing my cabbages?' he howled.

'Why, Mr. Man is stealing them,' said Brer Rabbit, 'didn't you know? I was passing your house just a while back and there was Mr. Man digging up all your cabbages and loading them into his cart.

'And I said to him I said: "Mr. Man, you can't take those cabbages. I have already arranged to buy them from Brer Fox myself and at a very fair price too."

'And Mr. Man, he said back to me, he said: "Brer Fox has been taking my chickens, so I'm taking his cabbages and

that's fair." So I said well some folks might call it fair and some folks might call it stealing, but I'm not going to stay a-arguing here.'

Then Brer Rabbit stopped for breath, for by this time Brer Fox was running up the road.

Brer Fox he ran all the way home and when he found that his cabbages were still growing in the ground and that there was no sign of Mr. Man, he felt mighty foolish.

He felt far too foolish to go back and face Brer Rabbit.

So Brer Rabbit was rid of Brer Fox for quite a while.

But that still left Brer Bear and Brer Wolf.

As soon as Brer Fox was out of sight, Brer Bear shifted from one foot to the other.

'Brer Rabbit,' he said. 'Did you by any chance happen to pass my home as you were trotting along away?'

Brer Rabbit looked at Brer Bear with great big eyes.

'Surely you aren't going to tell me that a clever fellow like you don't know what is going on at his own home?' he said, all innocent like.

Of course Brer Bear didn't want to appear foolish.

'O' course I know *all* that is going along at my house,' he said – 'er – I guess.'

'Of course you do,' agreed Brer Rabbit, 'and I think it is mighty fine of you to let your old lady paint the front door purple, like she is doing. Why, there's many a husband would be broken-hearted to see his house spoilt by having his front door painted that silly colour, but you're a mighty fine fellow to let your wife have her own way like that.'

You understand that Brer Rabbit knew full well that Brer Bear just hated purple.

It was his most unfavourite colour – it surely was.

So with no more ado, Brer Bear he upped and raced off home.

And when he found that his front door was the same old brown colour and that his old lady was shelling peas for dinner like always, he felt pretty stupid.

Far too stupid to go back and look Brer Rabbit in the eye and see how he was a-laughin'.

So Brer Bear, he slunk indoors and didn't bother Brer Rabbit for a week or two.

So only Brer Rabbit and Brer Wolf were left standing in the meadow.

But Brer Rabbit still had trouble, for Brer Wolf, he was a big fellow and mighty mean.

And by this time Brer Wolf was beginning to get a touch suspicious.

'And I suppose now you're a-goin' to tell me that there is something wrong at *my* home,' he said looking at Brer Rabbit – all sneery like.

'Oh no,' smiled Brer Rabbit, 'I did pass your home, but everything there is fine. I mean, I know what a clean, fussy chap you are. So when I saw the river overflowing and running straight through your house, I thought to myself I did, that Brer Wolf is going to be mighty pleased to see his floors washed over like that, and if some of his furniture is being carried away by the flood, why I know he'll think it well worth it to have a fresh washed house.'

But by this time Brer Wolf was hastening home and Brer Rabbit was free to go on his way without fear of being bothered by his big friends for quite a while to come.

A story about the little rabbits.

One day when Brer Rabbit was going visiting and Mrs. Rabbit was going shopping, all the little rabbits stayed at home and played in the field.

'Be good children,' called Mrs. Rabbit, as she went down the road. 'No mischief, now!'

Well, it happened that Brer Fox was coming around the bend in the road just as Mrs. Rabbit walked away.

He looked at the plump little rabbits as they played in the field, and he thought about his empty stewpot.

He thought and he thought and he said to himself:

'If I can make the little rabbits behave badly, or be disobedient, I will have a mighty excuse to put them in my stewpot for supper tonight.'

Brer Fox noticed a big stick of sugar cane standing in a corner of the field.

So he called out to the little rabbits:

'Now then, you young rabbits, break me off a fine piece of that sugar cane.'

Well now, Brer Rabbit and Mrs. Rabbit had raised their children to obey their elders and always do as they were told. So they all went over to the sugar cane and tried to break off a piece for Brer Fox.

They pulled and they wrestled and they puffed and they panted, but it was no use. They couldn't break that piece of sugar cane. They were too little.

And all the while Brer Fox kept calling to them to hurry.

So the little rabbits struggled and hustled some more, but they couldn't break the sugar cane.

34

They were mighty worried beca...se they couldn't do what they had been told to do.

Then their friend, the little bird, sang out from the branch of a nearby tree:

'*Use your teeth and gnaw it,*
Use your teeth and saw it.
Gnaw it and saw it,
And then you can break it.'

So the good little rabbits took their friend's advice and they gnawed and they sawed away at the sugar cane until they could break it.

Then they took the piece of sugar cane to Brer Fox.

That meant Brer Fox couldn't be cross with the little rabbits about the sugar cane, so he had to think of something else.

He looked around and saw an old bucket with lots of holes in the bottom.

'Come here, little rabbits!' he called. 'Take this bucket and run down to the stream and fetch me a drink of water.'

The little rabbits tried hard to do as they were told.

But as fast as they put water in the bucket, why, it ran straight out again through the holes in the bottom.

Then the same little bird flew by singing:

'*The bucket holds water same as a tray,*
If you fill it with moss and dab it with
    clay.
The fox will get crosser the longer you
    stay.
So fill it with moss and dab it with
    clay.'

In a moment the little rabbits had put some moss in the bottom of the bucket and smeared it over with wet clay from the banks of the stream.

And sure enough, the water stayed in the bucket, just as their friend had said it would.

They took a bucket of fresh water to Brer Fox, so that he could have a drink.

Brer Fox was really mad, I can tell you, because he had reckoned the little rabbits would never be able to bring him water in a bucket full of holes.

So he still had no reason to say that they were bad for not doing as they had been told to do.

So then Brer Fox sat and had a good think and he thought to himself:

'I'm bigger than the little rabbits. And I'm bigger than Brer Rabbit. I don't need an *excuse* to eat the baby rabbits. I can just *eat* them.'

It certainly was lucky for the little rabbits that their clever pa, Brer Rabbit came home right at that moment.

Brer Rabbit took one look at Brer Fox and knew what was in his mind.

Brer Rabbit was clever like that.

'Howdy, Brer Fox,' said Brer Rabbit, polite as can be.

'Howdy, Brer Rabbit,' replied Brer Fox, smiling all friendly like, as if there wasn't a bad thought in his wicked head.

'I see you've been a-chattin' to the baby rabbits,' went on Brer Rabbit.

'I surely have,' said Brer Fox, smiling more than ever, but somehow managing to look more and more frightening.

'We've had a lovely chat,' went on Brer Fox, 'in fact I enjoyed talking to the little rabbits so much I was a-thinkin' of asking them to walk home with me, just to help the weary way to pass more quickly with their pretty talking.'

Brer Rabbit didn't like the sound of that at all.

He knew where the road to Brer Fox's house would lead.

Straight into the stewpot.

But he didn't like to come right out and say so – what with Brer Fox being so big and all.

So Brer Rabbit said:

'That sure is a fine idea, Brer Fox, but I'm afraid *Mrs*. Rabbit wouldn't like it. You see tonight she has prepared a special onion and carrot stew for the little rabbits to eat and I happen to know that it's ready right at this very minute – it surely is.

'But,' went on Brer Rabbit, in his cunning way, 'tomorrow morning I'll send the baby rabbits over to chat with you Brer Fox. I always believe in being neighbourly, I surely do.'

Brer Fox thought for a moment, and he liked Brer Rabbit's plan.

After all, if the baby rabbits ate a meal of onions and carrots that night, tomorrow they would be plumper and more flavoursome than ever, so it was worth waiting for a day.

And as well as that, it would be rather difficult to catch all the rabbits and carry them off with Brer Rabbit interfering, as he was bound to do now.

But if Brer Rabbit would send the rabbits over to Brer Fox's house next day all on their own, why then, Brer Fox would be able to catch them with no trouble at all.

'That sounds a mighty fine plan, Brer Rabbit,' he said, 'but you do promise to send the little rabbits tomorrow, don't you.'

'Tomorrow, I will surely send them,' promised Brer Rabbit.

So Brer Fox went home at a fair clip, thinking he had been mighty cunning.

And Brer Rabbit took the little rabbits indoors and Mrs. Rabbit came home and they had onion and carrot stew and it was delicious.

And Brer Rabbit put the little rabbits to bed with hot drinks and he read them a story or two and put teddy bear to watch over them and told them never to chat to Brer Fox again, but to run away at the sight of him.

Well the next day Brer Fox looked out all day for the baby rabbits to arrive, but they never did.

So just before sunset Brer Fox stormed over to Brer Rabbit's house and demanded to know why Brer Rabbit hadn't sent the baby rabbits over as he had promised.

'Oh, but I didn't say I would send the baby rabbits over *today*,' smiled Brer Rabbit. 'I said I would send them over *tomorrow*.'

And then he added:

'Haven't you heard that saying, Brer Fox, *tomorrow never comes*.'

And he slammed the door shut and that was the end of that.

Brer Rabbit had won again.

The load of apples.

Now as we were saying before, these days, times are mighty different from what they used to be.

These days, when a rabbit sees a man, the rabbit runs off.

But in the old days Brer Rabbit was so clever that folk had to watch out for *him*.

There were many times when Brer Rabbit tricked Mr. Man – and this is the story of one of those times.

It happened when Mr. Man was driving his cart home along the road from the orchard. The cart was full of apples, big red round juicy apples.

When Brer Rabbit saw all those apples, he thought to himself: 'How is it Mr. Man has all those apples and my little rabbits have none at all to eat?'

And Brer Rabbit thought to himself that there was something mighty wrong about that.

So, by and by, Brer Rabbit called out: 'Howdy, Mr. Man. Can I have a ride in your cart, please sir?'

Mr. Man stopped his horse and he said: 'Howdy, Brer Rabbit. Why do you want a ride in my cart when you were going in the other direction?'

Brer Rabbit scratched himself on the back of his neck with his hind foot and said: 'Mr. Man, you don't know me very well to ask that question. Don't you know that I'm the kind of person who just likes to ride in a cart no matter which direction it is going in?'

So Mr. Man said that Brer Rabbit could have a ride in his cart. He tried to get Brer Rabbit to sit on the seat beside him, but Brer Rabbit said he was frightened of falling and lay in the back of the cart right on top of the pile of apples.

In a while they came to a steep hill and Mr. Man had to give all his attention to the horse. So Brer Rabbit tossed out a handful of apples.

Then they came to a bumpy bit of road and Mr. Man had to drive very carefully and while he wasn't looking Brer Rabbit tossed out several more handsful of apples.

Then they came to a sharp bend and the horse had to go slowly.

Mr. Man tightened the reins and while he was doing that, Brer Rabbit threw out some more apples.

Next they came to a place where the trees grew low over the road and Mr. Man had to bend right down so that the branches wouldn't knock his hat off his head.

And while he was doing that, Brer Rabbit tossed out yet more apples.

At last Mr. Man reached his house and went to the back of the cart to unload his apples – but there was Brer Rabbit lying all by himself in the middle of the empty cart.

'Where are my apples?' shouted Mr. Man.

Brer Rabbit pretended to be very surprised.

'Apples?' he asked innocently. 'What apples?'

'Why, the apples that were in the back of this cart,' yelled Mr. Man.

Brer Rabbit shook his head sadly.

'If I were you, Mr. Man,' he said, 'I would stop making a lot of fuss about apples or folk will think you are going out of your mind. There are no apples and there never were any apples. And you can't say I haven eaten your apples, because look at how flat and empty my tummy is.'

And with that Brer Rabbit walked off down the road.

Mr. Man stood there just mighty puzzled. Perhaps he had imagined the apples, because Brer Rabbit certainly hadn't eaten them.

But if Mr. Man had followed Brer Rabbit, he would have known that he *hadn't* imagined the apples.

They had been real enough.

Because there was Brer Rabbit picking them up from the road and taking them home to his family.

Brer Rabbit tells a funny story.

Back in the days when Brer Rabbit lived, there were no television sets.

In the long winter evenings, folks just sat round the fire trying to keep warm and told stories.

Well, one winter evening, Brer Rabbit and his little rabbits were sitting round the fire feeling mighty happy because they had eaten crumpets for tea. And there is nothing like a warm tummy full of buttered crumpets for making folks feel happy.

'Pa! Pa! Tell us a story,' chorused the baby rabbits.

And Brer Rabbit settled down in the armchair to tell a story about Grandfather Rabbit, who had lived way back in the days when the land had been quite wild, in the days before the roads had arrived.

'You see, in the old days there were roads leading from one important place to another, but there were no roads leading to the little country spots.

Maybe there was a footpath or two that folks could follow if they had sharp eyes, but mostly there was nothing.

And that was the way folks liked it.

Because in those days folks liked to mind their own business and expected other folk to do the same.

"I don't want to go anywhere bothering other folk and I don't expect other folk to come here bothering me," Grandfather Rabbit always used to say to his family.

So Grandfather Rabbit and his family

those rabbit thingummies live. I've never seen a rabbit, you know, being a city chap, but they tell me that rabbits like eating lettuce."

"That sure is right," replied Grandfather Rabbit, drawing himself up tall and folding his ears short and trying to look as much like a man as possible.

"So can you tell me of a nice meadow hereabouts where none of these rabbit chappies ever come," asked Mr. City Man.

"Well, this is a very nice meadow," smiled Grandfather Rabbit, pointing at the meadow next to the one where he and his family lived, "and only me and my family ever come here."

"Oh well, that's fine then," smiled Mr. City Man, "just so long as those rabbit fellows aren't about."

So Mr. City Man built a road up to the meadow next to where Grandfather Rabbit and his family lived.

It was a nice road, quite small and pretty, just wide enough for farm wagons.

And right soon a farmer came driving along the road and built himself a nice farm and started growing lettuces.

And when the lettuces were big and fat and juicy, they made mighty fine meals for Grandfather Rabbit and his family.

How they all did laugh when they thought about Mr. City Man asking Grandpa whether there were any rabbits living near the meadow.

Times were good for a long time with all those free lettuce about, but then of course, even city folk got to be able to recognize a rabbit when they saw one.'

'Ah well,' smiled Brer Rabbit. 'Good times can't last for ever, but Grandfather Rabbit sure knew how to make the best of a chance when he saw one.'

stayed living in the same old field and that was that.

But one day, a mighty smart fellow from the city came out building roads.

He didn't know much about country matters, so he stopped to ask some advice from Grandfather Rabbit.

Mind you, he did think that Grandfather Rabbit's face was mighty furry and his ears were on the long, pointy side, but then this fellow, who was Mr. City Man, knew that country folks were peculiar, so he thought nothing of it, nothing at all.

"Hey, you there," he called to Grandfather Rabbit, "I want to build a road leading to a meadow that would make a good lettuce farm. But I want to make sure the meadow is nowhere near where

Brer Rabbit
and
Brer Hawk.

Brer Rabbit was a mighty biggety sort of a rabbit. He didn't care what he said to anyone.

And he didn't care what fun he made of anyone.

All this acting biggety often got Brer Rabbit into real trouble.

And that's what happened one day when Brer Rabbit was hopping along the road singing a favourite song to himself.

He saw a shadow pass on the ground in front of him.

And he looked up and there was Brer Hawk, flying around and around in the sky above.

Well, if Brer Rabbit had been a sensible sort of person, he would have run mighty hard. Because Brer Hawk liked rabbit stew just as much as

Brer Fox and Brer Bear and Brer Wolf.

Brer Rabbit was feeling so biggety that he just went on hopping along and what's more he started to shout smart things up at Brer Hawk.

'Have the moths been eating your feathers, Brer Hawk?' he shouted. 'They sure look kind of chewed up.'

Brer Hawk said nothing. He just circled round and round.

Next Brer Rabbit threw sticks up at Brer Hawk.

'See if you can dodge these,' he laughed, 'or are you getting old and stiff, Brer Hawk?'

Brer Hawk, he said nothing. He just circled lower and lower.

Then Brer Rabbit put a stick to his shoulder and pretended the stick was a gun and said: 'Bang! BANG!'

Brer Rabbit was being far too cheeky, but Brer Hawk, he just circled lower and lower.

By and by he dropped straight down on to Brer Rabbit and grabbed hold of him and held him fast.

Well now, Brer Rabbit suddenly felt mighty foolish. He stood there without struggling and he thought and he thought about how he was going to escape from Brer Hawk.

'I was only having fun, Brer Hawk,' he said very politely. 'You don't need to make a bother about it.'

But Brer Hawk replied: 'You've been playing tricks for too long, Brer Rabbit. It's the stewpot for you now.'

'Will you let me do one important thing first?' asked Brer Rabbit.

'What is it?' squawked Brer Hawk.

'I have some gold hidden right over there under the corner of the fence,' said Brer Rabbit. 'My little rabbits must know where it is or they will go hungry when I am gone.'

'Show me where the gold is, Brer Rabbit,' said Brer Hawk. 'I will give it to your children after I have eaten you for dinner.'

Brer Hawk, of course, meant to keep the gold for himself.

'Very well,' said Brer Rabbit, 'I will dig up the gold for you to give to my baby rabbits, but I cannot dig while you are holding me so tight.'

So Brer Hawk, thinking that Brer Rabbit couldn't escape if he watched him closely, let Brer Rabbit loose to dig for the gold.

So Brer Rabbit started to dig under the corner of the fence and Brer Hawk perched on the fence and watched.

'Don't be too long about it, Brer Rabbit,' called Brer Hawk, 'I'm getting mighty hungry.'

'All right, all right,' replied Brer Rabbit, digging furiously into the soil. 'I'm being as quick as I can.'

He dug and he dug.

The hole got deeper and deeper.

Suddenly Brer Rabbit disappeared altogether.

'Where are you, Brer Rabbit?' called Brer Hawk into the hole.

'Here I am,' replied a voice.

Brer Hawk looked deeper down into the hole, but he still couldn't see Brer Rabbit.

'Where?' he asked again.

'Here,' laughed the voice and looking over the fence Brer Hawk saw that Brer Rabbit had dug right under the fence and come up in the middle of a briar patch, where no one could ever catch him.

And then Brer Hawk realized that there had never been any gold and that he had been tricked into letting Brer Rabbit escape. So he flapped his wings and flew away feeling mighty glum.

A Happy Christmas.

The first snows of winter had fallen and the weather was beginning to turn mighty chillsome like and suddenly all the animals started to think about Christmas.

But Brer Rabbit, he thought more than most.

He had to.

Because Brer Rabbit knew that if he didn't think mighty hard he and his family might end up as Christmas dinner for Brer Wolf or Brer Fox or Brer Bear.

So Brer Rabbit went out and spoke to his little baby rabbits as they were sliding in the meadow.

'I'm going to go a-calling on Brer Wolf and Brer Fox and Brer Bear,' he said, 'and after I have spoken to them, all you little rabs will be quite safe till after Christmas. But don't be surprised if Brer Fox and Brer Wolf and Brer Bear come a-looking at you. They might stare mighty hard, but they won't eat you none.'

So the baby rabs went on playing and Brer Rabbit he set off on his visiting.

Now as luck would have it, Brer Wolf and Brer Fox were all taking tea at Brer Bear's house.

And they were all discussing how they could catch Brer Rabbit and Mrs. Rabbit and all the little rabbits and eat them for Christmas.

'After all,' smiled Brer Bear, 'everyone wants a nice *big* dinner for Christmas, so we might as well eat the lot of them.'

'Sure thing!' agreed Brer Wolf, 'and if we cooked Brer Rabbit alone, he might feel lonely in the stewpot and we wouldn't want that, would we?'

'We surely wouldn't,' agreed Brer Fox, 'not at Christmas time, which is the season of goodwill.'

Well, just then, there came a rat-tat-tatting at the door.

And there was Brer Rabbit.

'Howdy!' smiled Brer Rabbit.

'Howdy!' replied Brer Bear and Brer

Wolf and Brer Fox in unison.

And they did have the grace to look a bit embarrassed, though why they should goodness knows, when they were planning to be so kind to Brer Rabbit.

Brer Rabbit glanced round at the three big animals.

'Having a nice little get-together?' he asked, all innocent like.

'Surely are,' smiled Brer Bear.

'Talking over Christmas plans, perhaps?' went on Brer Rabbit.

'Maybe,' grinned Brer Wolf

'Well,' said Brer Rabbit, 'I'm here to tell you that you needn't worry about your Christmas dinners, just so long as you don't mind waiting for them till the day after Christmas.'

Brer Bear and Brer Wolf and Brer Fox felt mighty surprised.

'How come?' they asked.

'Well,' said Brer Rabbit, 'I've been a-thinking and I've decided that I've been mighty selfish all these years.'

Brer Bear looked at Brer Wolf and Brer Wolf looked at Brer Fox.

They couldn't understand Brer Rabbit at all, not one little bit.

'Well,' said Brer Wolf, 'maybe you have and maybe you haven't. I don't wish to say rude things about a friend like you, you understand. But what has any of this got to do with our Christmas dinners?'

Brer Rabbit cleared his throat.

'I believe in plain speaking,' he said, 'and there's no denying that you good folks like rabbit stew. So what I thought was that as you have been such mighty good friends to me, I would make sure you all had fine big rabbit stews for your Christmas dinners.

'You see,' went on Brer Rabbit, I've noticed that Mrs. Rabbit has been getting in some nice tit-bits of food – mince pies, chocolates, nuts, puddings and suchlike, ready for Christmas.

'And I thought to myself, bless my buttons if Mrs. Bear and Mrs. Wolf and Mrs. Fox aren't doing just the same thing as my old lady and getting lots of fine tit-bits ready for Christmas.'

Brer Bear looked round at the others, and they all nodded.

It was true.

'So I thought,' said Brer Rabbit, 'what

a wonderful plan it would be if you, Brer Bear and you, Brer Wolf and you, Brer Fox gave me and my family all the nice tit-bits that your old ladies have bought.'

Brer Bear and Brer Wolf and Brer Fox stared at Brer Rabbit in amazement.

He certainly was talking mighty peculiar.

Just as if any of them was likely to give away their nice food to Brer Rabbit.

'Because, you see, I figured,' went on Brer Rabbit, 'that if me and my family ate all our tit-bits and all your tit-bits, it would make us so fat and juicy that all together we would make the most marvellous rabbit stew that ever was known. And that all you good folk would rather eat nothing much *before* Christmas and then have a simply spiffing meal on the day *after* Christmas.'

Brer Rabbit paused and glanced round.

Brer Bear was looking very interested.

Brer Wolf nodded. 'It makes sense,' he agreed.

Brer Fox was already licking his lips.

Brer Bear looked at Brer Wolf and Brer Wolf looked at Brer Fox.

They sure were mighty surprised.

Brer Bear rubbed at his ears and said:

'Would you mind repeating that last remark, Brer Rabbit. Do you know, for a moment there, I thought you said you wanted us to have rabbit stew for our Christmas dinners.'

'There's no need to go a-pounding your ears like that, Brer Bear,' said Brer Rabbit. 'There's nothing wrong with them. I *did* say that you should have rabbit stew for your Christmas dinner.'

Then Brer Rabbit went on:

'You see I fell to thinking and I thought – what good am I doing lounging around enjoying myself and eating up lettuce? That is all just plain selfish. If I were a decent chap, I would be turning myself into a good dinner for those fine fellows Brer Bear and Brer Wolf and Brer Fox.'

Brer Bear suddenly started to believe Brer Rabbit.

He stood up.

'Well, in that case,' he said, 'Why wait till Christmas? I'll get the stewpot out right now.'

That didn't suit Brer Rabbit at all. He took a hasty couple of steps nearer to the door.

But he went on talking.

He went on talking because he had some mighty clever plans afoot.

'No. No. Not *now*, Brer Bear,' he said. 'I couldn't be so mean as to let you eat me *now*. I am going to fatten myself up. In fact that is why I said I wanted you to wait till the day *after* Christmas before you have your rabbit stew Christmas dinner.'

So it was agreed that right up until Christmas day Brer Bear and Brer Wolf and Brer Fox would give all their nice Christmassy tit-bits to Brer Rabbit and his family.

And Brer Rabbit and his family would eat them all up – yes indeed.

And on Christmas day the rabbits would have their own Christmas dinner to make themselves really plump and full of good things.

'Then,' smiled Brer Rabbit, 'on the day after Christmas you folks can call round and eat everyone in the house.'

Brer Wolf and Brer Bear and Brer Fox were thrilled.

Brer Bear gave Brer Rabbit all the mince pies and nuts he had in the house.

And later on that day Brer Fox called

at Brer Rabbit's house and gave him a lovely parcel containing chocolates and raisins.

'Be sure to eat the raisins,' said Brer Fox. 'I love raisin-flavoured stew.'

Mrs. Rabbit and all the little rabbits were really thrilled at all the nice food being brought to their house.

Then right at tea time, Brer Wolf came knocking at the door.

'Here's some chocolate cake,' he smiled, handing over a beautiful cake with icing on the top.

Then he gave Brer Rabbit a saucepan with carrot stew and dumplings inside.

'Mrs. Wolf made this specially to save Mrs. Rabbit from over-working,' he smiled.

'Mrs. Wolf said she didn't want Mrs. Rabbit running round wearing herself to a shadow – not just before Christmas Heh! Heh!'

And so it went on day after day.

Mrs. Rabbit didn't have to do any more shopping or cooking. Good things to eat just kept arriving at the door by

the hour.

Mrs. Rabbit and the baby rabbits were mighty puzzled.

'How come Brer Bear and Brer Wolf and Brer Fox are being so good to us?' asked Mrs. Rabbit.

'I guess they are just naturally kind-hearted,' smiled Brer Rabbit.

'Hmm!' sniffed Mrs. Rabbit, 'That I will never believe. They are up to no good. You mark my words.'

Brer Rabbit smiled.

'Well, maybe they are up to no good,' he grinned, 'but *I* surely am up to *lots* of good. Just trust in me, Mrs. Rabbit.'

And knowing that Brer Rabbit was mighty clever, Mrs. Rabbit stopped worrying and just enjoyed all the good food that came her way.

But as Christmas drew closer, Brer Bear, he fell to thinking.

He fell to thinking that perhaps Brer Rabbit was up to his tricks.

So Brer Bear he called Brer Wolf and Brer Fox to a meeting and he said:

'Now, friends, I'm not one to think bad thoughts about my neighbours, but I can't help wondering if Brer Rabbit is trying to trick us.

'Supposing Brer Rabbit is taking all

this food from us, but when the time comes for him and his family to be turned into rabbit stew, they run away and don't let us catch them after all?'

Brer Wolf felt quite upset.

'Do you think he could be that sneaky?' he asked.

Brer Fox took a deep breath.

'Brer Bear is right,' he said, 'Brer Rabbit *could* be that sneaky and then some.'

'Well, then what shall we do?' asked Brer Wolf. 'If we stop giving the food to the rabbits, they will stop getting fat *and* they will know we suspect something.'

Brer Bear tapped his nose.

'Here is where we are just as cunning as Brer Rabbit,' he smiled. 'We will go on giving the rabbits the nice food, but we will take it in turns to watch their house. Between us we will watch it day and night – we won't give those rabbits the chance to sneak off and visit relatives for Christmas, or do whatever I'm sure Brer Rabbit has in mind.'

So that is what happened.

Morning, noon and night either Brer Bear or Brer Wolf or Brer Fox was outside the rabbits' home watching and watching with hardly a blink.

And Brer Rabbit he mighty soon noticed what was a-going on.

But Brer Rabbit, he wasn't bothered none.

Brer Rabbit, he went out and spoke to Brer Bear real friendly like.

'I see you've heard the same rumour as I have,' he smiled.

Brer Bear was real surprised.

'What rumour is that?' he asked.

'Why, that Father Christmas has built a workshop hereabouts and that if you watch real still and quiet you can see him with his sack of toys and his sledge slipping off to deliver some early Christmas presents,' said Brer Rabbit.

'Of course,' added Brer Rabbit hastily, 'there are no *reindeer* pulling the sledge. They don't come on duty till Christmas Eve.'

'Oh, of course not,' replied Brer Bear, not wishing to appear ignorant about these things and also not wishing to say he hadn't heard the rumour, otherwise Brer Rabbit might have asked him exactly why he *was* watching there.

But when later that evening Brer Bear, who was still on duty, saw a figure in a red coat and hood with a beard pulling a sledge with lots of sacks on it, he took no notice, because he felt sure it was Father Christmas.

The strange thing was that after 'Father Christmas' left, there was no more sign of the rabbits and certainly no rabbit stew for Brer Bear and Brer Fox and Brer Wolf. They never could understand how it happened and never found out to this day.

The barbecue.

The winter after Brer Rabbit's Christmas adventure was a very cold one.

By the time Brer Rabbit came back with his family from his relatives on the other side of the mountains, Brer Bear and Brer Wolf and Brer Fox had forgotten about being cheated of their Christmas rabbit stew.

Everything was back to normal except that food was short because of all the winter cold.

Even Brer Rabbit found it hard to keep full plates on the dinner table.

The only person in the whole land who had plenty of food was Mr. Man.

He always stored away enough food to last him through the winter and the springtime, too.

But, of course, Mr. Man didn't give any of his food to the animals.

It was quite the other way around. He stored his food away so carefully that the animals had no chance of getting hold of it.

Well, but there was one animal who reckoned he was smart enough to help himself to some of Mr. Man's food.

And that was Brer Rabbit.

Brer Rabbit looked into his larder and saw that the only food he had left was – two little potatoes.

So he put them in his pocket and went over to Mr. Man's house.

Now, you may think that was a mighty funny thing for Brer Rabbit to do – to take food to Mr. Man's house when he had plenty and Brer Rabbit had none.

But Brer Rabbit's smart little rabbity brain had worked out a plan.

When he came to Mr. Man's house, Brer Rabbit watched and waited until Mr. Man went out to work in the fields.

Then Brer Rabbit made a fire with dry sticks. He put some bricks on either side and some wire fencing over the bricks.

Then he put his two little potatoes to roast on the wire fencing.

By and by the roasting potatoes began to smell really delicious.

Mr. Man's little girl came out of the house.

She watched Brer Rabbit.

'Those potatoes sure smell nice,' said Mr. Man's little girl.

'Yes, indeed, there is no finer smell than the smell of roasting potatoes in the open air,' smiled Brer Rabbit in a mighty friendly way.

'In fact, everything cooked in the open air seems to smell and taste better than when it's cooked inside,' Brer Rabbit went on.

Mr. Man's little girl looked at the two little potatoes roasting over the fire and she knew that they were only just enough for Brer Rabbit, so she didn't like to ask if she could taste them.

So then Mr. Man's little girl said: 'Brer Rabbit, if I bring out one of the sausages I am going to have for my dinner will you be kind enough to roast it for me on your fire?'

Of course, this was just what Brer Rabbit wanted, but he pretended to think things over mighty serious for a bit.

Then he said: 'Well, seeing as you are such a nice little girl, I don't mind going to the bother of collecting a bit more wood and building a bit more fire and cooking your sausage for you. No,

I don't mind that. Don't mind at all.'

'Brer Rabbit, you are real kind,' smiled Mr. Man's little girl and she ran indoors and fetched a nice fat sausage.

Well, Brer Rabbit, he made a real fuss about building the fire up big and hot and he roasted that sausage and it surely smelt divine.

Mr. Man's little girl ate half of it and gave the other half to Brer Rabbit for being so kind.

The sausage sure tasted good to Brer Rabbit, yes indeed.

The sausage tasted very nice to Mr. Man's little girl as well.

'Oh, how I wish Daddy could taste sausages cooked on an open fire like this," she sighed. 'I know he would enjoy them so much more than the sausages we cook indoors.'

'Why how strange that you should say that,' gasped Brer Rabbit. 'Do you know I have been walking about for days and days thinking what a fine man your

pa is and wondering to myself just what I could do to make him happy.'

'Really?' said Mr. Man's little girl.

She had never heard her father say Brer Rabbit was in the habit of doing him good turns.

Still, it was nice to know that there was much more good in people than you knew.

'Why, if you like,' went on Brer Rabbit, 'I could build this fire up even hotter and cook your daddy's dinner for him, so he could taste how delicious food cooked in the open really is.'

Mr. Man's little girl was thrilled. She liked to please her daddy.

She ran into the house and she brought out lots of big fat sausages and some big fat carrots.

'Can you manage to cook all these?' she asked.

'Yes, indeed,' replied Brer Rabbit.

And his rabbity eyes gleamed and his mouth watered eagerly.

Mr. Man's little girl gave the sausages and the carrots to Brer Rabbit and he put them over his fire to roast with the potatoes.

My, they did smell good!

Then, who should come lolloping along, but one of Brer Rabbit's own children.

'Hallo, Daddy Rabbit,' said the baby rabbit, 'I just passed Mr. Man in the field and he said that he could smell such a fine smell that he didn't want to wait till dinner time, he wanted to eat now.'

Of course Mr. Man hadn't really said that at all.

It was all part of Brer Rabbit's plan to get some of Mr. Man's food.

'So Mr. Man wants something to eat now, does he?' smiled Brer Rabbit. 'Well, then perhaps his little girl would like to take this dinner out to him in the fields.'

Mr. Man's little girl shook her head.

'I'm not allowed to go out into the fields,' she said. 'I have to stay right here near the house.'

And that was just what Brer Rabbit wanted her to say.

'Don't worry,' he smiled, 'I couldn't stand by and not give help to my good friend, Mr. Man. *I* will take the food out to your daddy in the field.'

Mr. Man's daughter was very grateful.

'That is kind of you,' she smiled and she wrapped the hot food up in a clean cloth and gave it to Brer Rabbit.

Then she waved while Brer Rabbit and his little rabbit hopped away over the fields with all the nicely roasted food.

But, of course, Brer Rabbit and the baby rabbit didn't go anywhere near Mr. Man.

They went straight home and put the food on the table for themselves and Mrs. Rabbit and the other baby rabbits.

For a while Brer Rabbit was bothered about the way he had tricked the nice little girl.

He wondered if Mr. Man would be cross with her when he found out what had happened.

Then he reckoned that *he* wouldn't get mad at any of his family, if they were only doing their best to give him a nice meal.

So he decided that Mr. Man wouldn't get cross with *his* little girl.

Mrs. Rabbit was very pleased when she saw the food.

'Oh, my! What a lovely surprise,' she said, 'where did you get it?'

Brer Rabbit and the little rabbit laughed as they told her how they had tricked the Man family.

And the rabbit family certainly enjoyed their feast because they were

very hungry, very hungry indeed.

And when Mr. Man came home and found out how Brer Rabbit had tricked him out of his dinner, he was mighty cross at *first*.

Then he thought to himself:

'I have plenty of food, so I guess I can spare a little for that tricky rabbit.'

Because sometimes Mr. Man just had to admire how clever Brer Rabbit's tricks were.

So Mr. Man fetched out some more food and piled wood on to Brer Rabbit's fire and cooked the food out there in the open.

Then he and the little girl ate it for their dinner and it was mighty tasty.

'We must eat food cooked like this again,' smiled Mr. Man. 'But not when Brer Rabbit is about.'

Will o' the Wisp.

One year it happened that Brer Rabbit grew a mighty fine crop of onions in his garden and he kept boasting about them.

He boasted and he bragged and he acted mighty biggety in front of all the other animals and they decided to teach him a lesson.

Well, the day came when Brer Rabbit was due to take his onions to market and on that day Mrs. Rabbit happened to glance out of the window.

'Oh my,' she called to Brer Rabbit, mighty flustered, 'I can see Brer Bear just along the road and he's carrying a big heavy club.'

Then one of the little rabbits called out: 'Daddy, I can see Brer Wolf just along the road and he's carrying a long rope.'

And then Brer Terrapin arrived and said: 'I just passed Brer Fox along the road and he has his biggest stewpot with him.'

So one way and another Brer Rabbit decided not to go to market right then. He thought of a plan instead.

He asked Mrs. Rabbit to sit in the sun by the garden gate and if Brer Bear or Brer Wolf or Brer Fox asked about the onions, she was to say that Brer Rabbit wasn't going to market because he had

sold the onions to Will o' the Wisp, who would be collecting them directly.

Sure enough, in a little while Brer Bear and Brer Wolf and Brer Fox came nosing around.

'Where is Brer Rabbit?' they asked.

'Indoors with a headache,' replied Mrs. Rabbit.

'When is he going to take his onions to market?' asked Brer Fox.

'He isn't,' said Mrs. Rabbit.

'Why not?' asked Brer Wolf.

'Because Will o' the Wisp has bought them and he is coming to collect them at any minute now.'

Well now, it is a well-known thing that all the animals were mighty scared of Will o' the Wisp and Brer Bear and

Brer Wolf and Brer Fox wondered if Brer Rabbit was tricking them.

But *then* – they heard a clank-clanking that came nearer and nearer and the nearer it came the scarier it got.

Then round the corner came a character who shone and shimmered all over like the sun and who clanked and clattered something terrible.

Brer Bear and Brer Wolf and Brer Fox ran straight off home, thinking it was Will o' the Wisp.

But of course, it was Brer Rabbit draped all over with Mrs. Rabbit's saucepan lids.

'Well,' he smiled, 'I reckon as how it's time to take my onions to market now. Ho! Ho!'

Mrs. Lion finds Mr. Woodman.

One evening when Brer Rabbit was tucking his little rabbits up in bed, they asked him to tell them a story.

So he told them the story about the Woodman and Mrs. Lion – and this is it.

'Once upon a time, Mrs. Lion started acting mighty grand.

She acted so grandly that she went all round the neighbourhood saying what a mighty fine lioness she was.

But everywhere she went, she heard nothing but talk of Mr. Woodman.

Right in the middle of Mrs. Lion's boasting, someone would come up and say what a clever thing Mr. Woodman had done.

Mrs. Lion would say that she had done this – and then someone else would say how Mr. Woodman had done that and done it very well.

Mrs. Lion grew very, very tired of it and in the end she said she would find this Mr. Woodman and give him a good beating, just to show which of them was boss.

The other animals, they all told Mrs. Lion to leave Mr. Woodman alone.

But Mrs. Lion took no notice at all.

She set off along the highway and after a while she came upon Mr. Steer, grazing at the side of the road.

Mrs. Lion said: "Howdy!" in a most polite way.

And Mr. Steer likewise bowed low to show his good manners.

"Is there anyone around these parts called Mr. Woodman?" asked Mrs. Lion.

"To be sure there is," said Mr. Steer, "anyone will tell you that. I know him well myself."

"Well, I've come a long way to give him a good beating," said Mrs. Lion, "I'm going to show him who's boss."

"Well, if that's your idea," said Mr. Steer, "you had better have another think. You can see how big I am and how big my horns are. Well, that doesn't make any difference to Mr. Woodman. He comes right along here and he catches me and makes me pull a cart for him. You would do better to leave Mr. Woodman alone."

Mrs. Lion didn't agree. She went on along the road till she met up with Mr. Horse.

She asked Mr. Horse if he knew Mr. Woodman.

"I know him mighty well," said Mr. Horse. "What do you want with Mr. Woodman?"

"I'm hunting him to give him a beating," said Mrs. Lion.

Mr. Horse shook his head. "I wouldn't do that if I were you, Mrs. Lion," he said. "Mr. Woodman is mighty smart. You can see how big and strong I am, but Mr. Woodman can make me pull his plough for him. I think you should leave Mr. Woodman alone."

She went on until she saw someone in a field cutting logs to make a fence.

It was Mr. Woodman, but as Mrs. Lion had not seen Mr. Woodman before, she didn't know who it was.

Mr. Woodman was splitting logs and putting a wedge in to keep the split open.

"Howdy!" said Mrs. Lion. "Do you know Mr. Woodman?"

Mr. Woodman said he knew him as well as he knew his twin brother.

"Well, I want to find this Mr.

Woodman and give him a good beating," said Mrs. Lion, mighty grandly.

So Mr. Woodman said that if Mrs. Lion would put her paw into the split log to hold it open until he got back, he would fetch Mr. Woodman.

So Mrs. Lion marched up and she slapped her paw into the split.

Then Mr. Woodman knocked out the wedge and there was Mrs. Lion's paw held fast in the split!

"Well now, Mrs. Lion," said Mr. Woodman with a big smile, "I am the Mr. Woodman you want to beat, but I think I'll beat you instead."

And he did.

Mrs. Lion had such a lesson that to this day you will never find a lioness who is willing to go up to a man chopping logs and put her paw in the split in the log!'

And that was the end of the story that Brer Rabbit told.

The baby rabbits thought it was a mighty fine story.

'Thank you, Pa,' they said – and went straight to sleep.

Brer Fox
waters
the
lettuces.

It happened one summer, in the land where Brer Rabbit lived, that the weather suddenly became very hot.

The sun burned down and the land dried up and Brer Rabbit's lettuces looked mighty poorly, mighty poorly indeed.

'If I don't water those lettuces today, they will surely die,' thought Brer Rabbit.

He took a bucket and stood peering down into the rainwater barrel that stood at the side of his house.

'It's going to be mighty hard work hauling buckets of water out of this old rainwater barrel,' thought Brer Rabbit.

'And I'm going to be mighty tired by the time I'm through,' he thought, staring at the water.

Just at that moment Brer Fox happened to be loping by. He saw Brer Rabbit staring down into the barrel and he called out:

'Why are you staring into your rainwater barrel, Brer Rabbit?'

And, as quick as a flash, that smart Brer Rabbit replied:

'Why, I'm looking for a fine diamond ring that belongs to Mrs. Rabbit.'

'How did Mrs. Rabbit's fine diamond ring get into your rainwater barrel?' asked Brer Fox.

'Mrs. Rabbit let it slip off her finger as she was fetching water,' explained Brer Rabbit.

Brer Fox came across and he stared into the barrel, too.

Inside it was mighty black and dark.

'I can't see any diamond ring, Brer Rabbit,' said Brer Fox.

'Neither can I, Brer Fox,' said Brer Rabbit.

'How are you going to get it back then?' asked Brer Fox.

'I'm going to empty out all the water with this bucket. Then I'll find the ring at the bottom of the barrel,' said Brer Rabbit.

'Then why don't you get on with it?' asked Brer Fox.

'I will, Brer Fox, I will. But I was spending a happy moment thinking about what I would buy myself with the reward my wife has promised to give the person who finds her ring,' said Brer Rabbit.

'Reward?' asked Brer Fox.

'Yes, indeed,' said Brer Rabbit, 'Mrs. Rabbit has said that she will give a quarter of the value of the ring to the person who will get her ring back for her.'

Now the quarter of the value of a diamond ring is a mighty fine sum of money and Brer Fox fell to thinking of how many nice new jackets and how many fancy shirts he could buy with such a great sum.

At once Brer Fox, he snatched the bucket from Brer Rabbit's hands and pushed him aside and said.

'I'm going to scoop out that water and find that ring and claim that reward. And if you know what's good for you Brer Rabbit, you won't try to stop me.'

Well, Brer Rabbit, he hung his head and looked mighty glum.

'There's no justice in this world, when you can cheat me out of a fine reward just because you are bigger than I am,' he groaned. 'But I suppose I shall just have to put up with seeing you get the better of me, Brer Fox.'

Brer Fox grinned.

'You surely will,' he said and scooped out a bucket of water and slopped it on to the lawn.

But Brer Rabbit called out: 'Don't pour the water on the lawn, Brer Fox, Mrs. Rabbit gets mighty angry at muddy footmarks in the house. She won't give you a reward if you make the lawn right outside the door muddy. Take the water over there by the lettuces, right away from the house.'

'All right, all right,' puffed Brer Fox. 'I don't care where the water goes, as long as it goes.'

And he ran about so fast between the barrel and the lettuces, that poor Brer Rabbit came over all hot just watching him.

Immediately the lettuces began to stand up nice and straight.

'I'm nearly at the bottom of the barrel, Brer Rabbit,' puffed Brer Fox, 'I should find that ring pretty soon now.'

'Yes indeed,' said Brer Rabbit as he strolled quietly into his house and locked all the doors and windows.

It was a good thing he did!

Brer Fox was so mad when he guessed that Brer Rabbit had tricked him into watering the lettuces that he shouted at Brer Rabbit for the rest of the day. But Brer Rabbit was safe indoors.

Brer Rabbit and the hot pies.

One day, when times were mighty hard, Brer Rabbit and Brer Fox fell in to walking together along the road.

Suddenly Brer Rabbit stopped and sniffed.

Brer Fox stopped too and asked what was the matter.

'I'm sure I smelled the most delicious smell,' replied Brer Rabbit.

And sure enough in a moment they heard a voice calling: 'Tasty hot pies for sale.' And a pieman came round the corner pushing a barrow of hot pies.

Brer Fox fished about in his pockets and found two or three small coins. Brer Rabbit did the same, but he only managed to find one or two.

They didn't even have enough money to buy one pie between them.

He began to think very hard indeed because he knew that pretty quickly the pieman would go and his pies with him.

He turned to Brer Fox.

'Of course, I know where there's a little store of money,' he said wistfully.

'It's a pity knowing where money is when you can't use it.'

'And why can't you use it?' asked Brer Fox greedily.

'Because it isn't mine, Brer Fox,' replied Brer Rabbit. 'I only discovered about this little store the other day and I can't take it if it isn't mine, can I?'

'Well, now, I don't know,' said Brer Fox. 'I mean, you might say it was just borrowing, because we do need those hot pies so badly on account of times being hard and all. Perhaps we ought to borrow that money, Brer Rabbit.'

'Do you really think so?'

Well by this time the pieman was going down the road away from them, but Brer Fox could still smell the pies and they smelled delicious.

'Yes, Brer Rabbit. I don't think anyone would mind if you borrowed that little store of money. I know *I* wouldn't mind.'

'Very well, if you say so,' grinned Brer Rabbit and he ran off to Brer *Fox*'s house, where the other day he had seen Brer Fox putting money in a piggy bank.

Brer Rabbit grabbed the piggy bank and with a knife emptied all the pennies out. Then he took them and ran back to Brer Fox.

They were just in time to buy some delicious hot pies and eat them.

Several weeks later, when times were better and Brer Fox had a penny to spare he picked up his piggy bank to put another penny in.

Of course it was empty – and then Brer Fox guessed that this must have been the little store of money Brer Rabbit had taken.

He was furious – but he had said himself that it was all right to take the money, so there was nothing he could do.

Brer Fox
runs a two minute mile.

One year nothing would grow right in Brer Rabbit's garden and he had mighty little to eat.

But that same year everything went right in Brer *Fox*'s garden and he had plenty to eat and enough left over to fill his store shed.

Brer Rabbit stood outside Brer Fox's shed feeling mighty envious.

'Aren't you afraid of folks stealing this delicious food you have in here?' he asked.

'No,' replied Brer Fox, 'first I have locked the door and the key is in my pocket and second I can run mighty fast and I will catch anyone who tries to steal anything.'

'But I have heard tell,' said Brer Rabbit, 'there are folks round here, who can run a two minute mile. Don't you think I should fetch my watch and test you to see if you can run a two minute mile, Brer Fox? You want to know if you can catch up with any two minute milers who try to steal your food.'

'Yes, you do that thing,' agreed Brer Fox, beginning to feel worried.

So Brer Rabbit ran home to fetch his

watch and when he got there, he told his baby rabbits to bring some sacks and baskets and hide themselves in the trees near Brer Fox's shed.

Then Brer Rabbit, watch in hand, ran back to join Brer Fox again.

'Right!' cried Brer Rabbit. 'It's just a mile round the big field and back through the pine wood. Are you ready?'

'Yes,' said Brer Fox.

'Are you steady?' asked Brer Rabbit.

'Steady!' cried Brer Fox.

'Then off you go!' said Brer Rabbit.

Brer Fox had only gone a few steps when Brer Rabbit cried out:

'Stop, Brer Fox! You can't possibly run with your *coat* on. Leave it here with me.'

Well, Brer Fox was so anxious to prove he could run a mile in two minutes

that he didn't even think about the key in his coat pocket.

Tossing off his coat, he raced off again.

Of course, the moment Brer Fox was out of sight, Brer Rabbit took the key from the jacket pocket and opened the shed.

Out from the trees ran the baby rabbits with their sacks and baskets at the ready.

It certainly didn't take them two minutes to fill their sacks and baskets with all those juicy carrots and turnips and by the time Brer Fox came puffing back, there was no sign of Brer Rabbit, no sign of his children and no sign whatever of any food.

All Brer Fox found was his coat and an open shed door.

And Brer Fox felt mighty silly.